There's a Wolf in my Pudding

David Henry Wilson was born in London and educated at Dulwich College and Pembroke College, Cambridge. He lectures at the universities of Bristol and Konstanz, West Germany, where he founded the student theatre. He and his wife live in Taunton, Somerset, and two of his three children are now at university. His children books have been translated into several languages and many of his plays have been produced in England and abroad, the best-known being his comedy *Gas and Candles*.

Jonathan Allen is himself a writer with an original and bizarre sense of humour, as well as an exceptionally talented illustrator. When not writing or drawing, he plays bass guitar in a pop group. He lives in London.

Other books by David Henry Wilson in Piccolo

Do Goldfish Play the Violin?
Elephants Don't Sit on Cars
The Fastest Gun Alive
How to Stop a Train with One Finger

There's a Wolf in my Pudding

There's

in my

Twelve Twisted
and Gruesome

Piper Books   published by Pan

a Wolf Pudding

Tortured, Grim Tall and Terrible Tales

by David Henry Wilson

drawings by Jonathan Allen

*For Carmen and Paco, Rolf and Christa, Joan and
Jean, Colin and Claudine, Linda and Jean-Pierre,
and Irmgard — wherever she is.*

First published 1986 by J. M. Dent & Sons
This Piper edition published 1988 by
Pan Books Ltd, Cavaye Place, London SW10 9PG
9 8 7 6 5 4 3 2 1
Text © David Henry Wilson 1986
Illustrations © Jonathan Allen 1986
All rights reserved
ISBN 0 330 29900 X
Printed and bound in Great Britain by
Richard Clay Ltd, Bungay, Suffolk

Contents

Little Red Riding Hood: the Wolf's Story

OK, so I got killed in the end and you all said yippee. I'm not complaining about that. I wasn't as clever as I thought I was, so I'll take my defeat like a wolf. But now that I'm a was-wolf (that is, a dead wolf), and I'm up here in Valhowla (paradise for wolves), I'll rest a lot easier if the record is set straight. The official accounts of what happened that day are all lies, and I hate lies — especially lies about me. So here's the story of what really happened.

The first lie that annoys me is all this big-bad-wolf business. Big? I may have been average size once, but by the time I was killed, I was more ribs than muscles. I hadn't had a decent meal in weeks. Skinny, yes — big, no. And why bad? What was ever bad about me? I reckon I'm one of the nicest wolves I know. So instead of, *In the forest there lived a big bad wolf*, now read, *In the forest there lived a skinny nice wolf*.

Next we come to the question of motive. The history books say I wanted to eat Little Red Riding Hood. I didn't, and I can prove it. But even if I *had* wanted to eat her, what's so terrible about that? When she had eggs and bacon for breakfast, did anyone complain that big bad Red Riding Hood took the eggs from the chicken as well as two slices off Porky Pig? When she had roast turkey for Christmas, did it bother her what might have happened to Mrs Turkey and all the little Turks? When she sank her teeth into a juicy rump

8

steak, did she spare a thought for some poor cow walking round the field with half its bottom missing? What's the difference between a little girl eating me and my mates, and me eating a little girl?

Anyway, as I said, I didn't want to eat her. Here's the proof. You remember she and I had a little chat in the woods? I asked her where she was going, what she had in the basket, and where her sick granny lived. Well, if I was close enough to talk to her, you'll have to agree that I was close enough to eat her. Why didn't I? Some of the accounts suggest it was because there were some woodcutters nearby. Rubbish. If there'd been a single woodcutter nearby, I'd have been off faster than you can say, "The wonderful wolf went away from the wood."

The fact is, I was after Red Riding Hood's basket with all the goodies in it. With my blunt old teeth I couldn't even bite a chicken, let alone a little girl. It was the basket I wanted. I thought of stealing it from her there and then, but for three reasons I didn't. First, I didn't want to upset her. Second, she might have started screaming, and I don't like screams, or people who hear screams. And third, she might not have let go, and I was in no condition for a fight.

9

My plan was very simple. I intended to pop along to Granny's cottage, give her a little scare so she'd run away for a few minutes, pretend I was Granny, and relieve Red Riding Hood of the basket. Then she would have gone home thinking she'd done her good deed, Granny would have come back feeling pleased she'd escaped from the wolf, and I'd have got the basket. We'd all have lived happily ever after.

Only things didn't quite work out that way. First of all, in spite of what the official reports might say, Granny wasn't there. I pushed open the door, all set to say "boo" and get out of the way as she rushed out, but there was nobody to say "boo" to. Actually, I was rather glad, because some grannies don't scare easily. I've seen grannies that scared me a good deal more than I scared them. Anyway, the room was empty, so I reckoned it was my lucky day. I crawled into bed, pulling the covers over me.

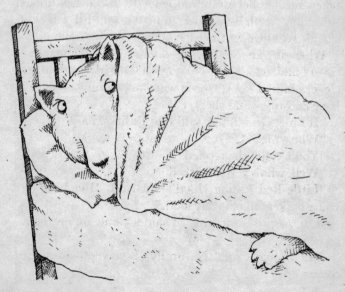

In a few minutes, Little Red Riding Hood came along, and again the history books have got it all wrong. Unless she was as short-sighted as a one-eyed rhinoceros, do you honestly think she would have taken me for her grandmother? All those lies about 'what big teeth you have', and so on. I'll tell you exactly what we said to each other.

When she knocked at the door, I stayed under the covers and called out: "Who is it?" (That was rather clever of me. I knew who it was, but Granny wouldn't have known, would she?)

"It's me, Grandma!" said Red Riding Hood.

"Who's me?" I asked.

"You's you!" she replied.

"Well, who's you?" I asked.

"Little Red Riding Hood!" she said. "I've brought you a basket full of lovely food."

"Oh, surprise, surprise!" I said. "Come in, my dear, come in."

And in she came. Naturally, I stayed under the covers.

"How are you, Grandma?" she asked.

"I'm not well at all, dear," I said. "I've caught a catching illness, and as I don't want you to catch it, too, I'll stay under the covers till you've gone. Just leave the basket there, dear, and run along home. Run quickly, 'cos I've heard there's a big bad wolf in the forest."

It was brilliant. I felt like jumping out of bed and giving myself a round of applause.

"Yes, Grandma," said Red Riding Hood, and she put down the basket, turned round to leave, and . . . just my luck! Who should walk into the room at that moment but Granny herself! I knew I was in trouble as soon as I heard the footsteps. I'd have made a run for it if I hadn't been paralysed with terror.

"Hullo, Red Riding Hood," said Granny.

"Hullo, Grandma," said Red Riding Hood.

"Hullo, trouble," said I to myself.

"Grandma," said Red Riding Hood, "if you're here, who could that be in your bed?"

I wished I could just curl up and disappear down the side of the mattress.

"Whoever you are," said Granny, "I've got you covered. Come out with your hands up."

I poked my nose out from under the blanket.

"Look," I said, "it's all been a terrible mistake . . ."

"It's the big bad wolf!" said Red Riding Hood.

"No, no," I said, "I'm just a skinny nice wolf . . ."

BANG, BANG, BANG!

Oh, the injustice! All I wanted was something to eat, but before I even had a chance to impress them with my charm and good intentions, Granny had put three bullets right where I should have had the fruit cake and chocolate biscuits. I collapsed like a chopped tree.

"Good shooting, Grandma!" said Red Riding Hood — though what was good about it I shall never know.

"Quick, fetch the vet!" I gasped.

But the last thing those two had in mind was to help poor dying Wolfie.

"We ought to get the newspapers here," said Granny. "This could be quite a story."

"Oh, yes," said Red Riding Hood. "They might publish our pictures and we'd be famous!"

And while I lay there, half in and half out of the world, they calmly discussed the tale they would tell the reporters. Granny was worried that she might get into trouble because she didn't have a licence for her gun. (I wish she'd thought of that earlier.) Red Riding Hood also wondered why Granny hadn't been in her bed, because she was supposed to be sick. It turned out that Granny had been on the lavatory, but she certainly wasn't going to tell *that* to the reporters.

"And what," said Granny, "are they going to think when they find the wolf in my bed? After all, I've got my reputation to think of."

"Blow your reputation," I groaned. "What about me? I've been shot!"

"You keep out of this, Wolfie," said Granny. "You've caused enough trouble as it is."

I'd caused trouble! Was it my fault she'd been on the lavatory? And who fired the gun? And who didn't have a licence? But it was no use arguing — they'd made up their minds that I was the villain and they were the heroes.

"Perhaps," said Red Riding Hood, "we can pretend someone else shot him — a hunter, or a woodcutter."

"But that wouldn't explain how he got into my bed," said Granny.

"I know what," cried Red Riding Hood. "We could say you were in bed, and Wolfie came in and ate you."

"You must be joking," I moaned. "With my teeth I couldn't even eat a chicken, let alone a tough old bird like Granny."

"Keep quiet, Wolfie!" said Granny. "No, the problem there, my dear, is that if he'd eaten me, I'd be dead. And I'm not."

"Well," said Red Riding Hood, "we could say he ate you whole, and then the woodcutter cut him open and you came out alive."

"Now that's an idea!" said Granny.

"Oh, yeah!" I gasped. "A newborn fifteen-stone sixty-year-old baby! Who's going to believe that?"

"Then," continued the Little Red Liar, "we'll say he disguised himself as you, I came in, and the woodcutter rescued me in the nick of time."

"Oh, well," I groaned, "why don't I eat a whole Red Riding Hood for dessert — make a proper meal of it?"

"Why not?" asked Granny.

"You're both crazy!" I panted. "Nobody in this whole wide world can be stupid enough to swallow a story like that!"

Those were my last words. With one more bullet from Granny, I huffed my last puff. But I died happy in the knowledge that nobody in the whole wide world could be stupid enough to swallow a story like that. Ugh, how wrong can a wolf be?

The Frog Prince Fashion

Once upon a time there was a princess who lost her favourite ball in a spring. Along came a frog saying he'd fetch it on condition that he could eat from her golden plate and sleep for three nights in her bed. The Princess wasn't too keen on the arrangement, but as she did want her ball back, she agreed. After three nights the frog turned into a handsome prince, they got married, and lived happily ever after. And that was how the trouble started. From that day on, girls all over the country started throwing balls into streams and offering board and lodging to the nearest frog. The result was a lot of rich ball-makers, a lot of fat frogs, and a lot of disappointed girls.

The story of the Frog Prince eventually reached France, and it wasn't long before French streams were full of lost balls, and French beds were full of fat frogs. After three nights French frogs remained just as froggy as English frogs, and so French girls remained as princeless as English girls. In most cases the third morning would see a few tears from the girl and a quick exit by the frog. But in a region called Provence, there would be screams of terror and a quick exit by the girl. The cause of the terror was a wicked witch named Grenwee.

Up until the age of the Frog Prince fashion, Grenwee had had a very unsuccessful career. In fact she had always been bottom of every league table published in *Witch* magazine. The reason for her lack of success was the fact that she could only perform one trick, which was to turn herself into a frog — and turning herself into a frog had proved to be utterly useless from every point of view. She had been on the verge of retiring from French witchery and emigrating to a country called Chad (where chadpoles come from), when suddenly frogs became all the rage. Overnight — or at least over three nights — Grenwee went from total failure to glorious success. Not only did she get herself free dinners and free bedding, but every third morning she would change herself back into a witch and scare the living daylights out of her hostess. Grenwee became the envy of all witches — and the terror of all would-be princesses.

News of Grenwee's wickedness at last reached the ears of the King of France. He himself had a daughter, and as he certainly didn't want her sleeping with frogs let alone with witches, he summoned his Minister for Frogging Affairs, Maître de Kweezeen, to see what could be done. Maître de Kweezeen consulted his colleagues, his friends, and his family, but finally found the answer in an old Voodoo-It-Yourself book of black magic.

"There's only one way to stop Grenwee," he informed the King. "But it's rather nasty."

"It couldn't be nastier than she is," said the King. "Tell me what it is, and I'll do it."

"You can't," said Maître de Kweezeen.

"Of course I can," said the King. "Kings can do anything."

Then the Minister explained that the task had to be performed by a princess or it wouldn't work, and the King had to agree that as there weren't many princesses with deep voices, bald heads and beards, perhaps he couldn't do it after all.

"Princess Gourmande will have to do it," he said, after hearing the full list of instructions. "She won't like it, but she's the only princess we've got."

The Princess said "Ugh!" several times when she heard what she had to do, but although she was very fat and very lazy, she was also brave and kind-hearted.

"If that's what must be done," she said, "then that's what I shall do." And at once she went off to the palace kitchen, which was where she spent most of her spare time, anyway. After a quick snack of fish soup, steak and onions, chocolate gâteau, camembert cheese and a cup of coffee, she gave cook the instructions that Mâitre de Kweezeen had handed over to her: cook was to prepare salt, pepper, milk, flour, butter, parsley, olive oil, chives, lemon juice and garlic, and leave them all right next to the oven.

"I don't think that'll fill you up, Your Highness," said the cook.

"I've never found anything that did," said the Princess.

Next, Princess Gourmande took the biggest, sharpest knife she could see in the kitchen, and carried it off to her bedroom, where she hid it under her pillow. And then she went with her favourite ball down to the spring at the bottom of the palace garden. She threw it up and down a few times, and then deliberately let it fall with a loud splash into the water.

"Oh dear!" she cried. "I've lost my favourite ball. Dear me, boo hoo, golly gosh and all that, who's going to get it for me?"

"I will!" cried a handsome young gardener, who'd been watching from behind a rose-bush, and before Princess Gourmande could stop him, he had dived into the stream and rescued the ball.

"Oh!" said the Princess. "Well, thank you very much."

"Not at all, Your Highness," said the gardener. "Glad to be of service."

He went back to his roses, and Gourmande waited for ten minutes before she tried again.

"Oh, goodness gracious me!" she said. "My favourite ball has fallen into the . . ."

But before she could finish her sentence, the young gardener had dived in again and rescued the ball.

"Thank you again," said the Princess.

"Any time, Your Highness," said the gardener, and went back to his roses.

This happened five times. Princess Gourmande enjoyed watching the gardener jump in and out of the water, but she knew this was hardly the way to catch a witch. As for the gardener, he didn't really enjoy jumping in and out of the water, but he began to wonder if perhaps this was the way to catch a princess. And when Gourmande invited him to go for a little walk in the garden, he had a feeling that before long he might well become more than just a gardener.

"Listen," said the Princess, when they were some distance away from the stream, "I'm trying to catch a wicked witch, and if you keep diving into the spring, I'll never catch her. So next time I throw my ball in, would you please stay away."

The handsome young gardener turned as red as a rose and said he was very sorry. The Princess said it was all right, and at any other time she'd love to watch him jump in and out of the water. The gardener said, "Well, how about tomorrow?" And the Princess said tomorrow would be fine. Then the gardener went off to his flower-beds, and the Princess went off to the spring where once again she threw in her ball and cried, "Oh, good heavens above, my favourite ball! Now what am I going to do?"

"Arrk, arrk!" said a voice from the bank of the spring. "I'll get it for you, Princess, on one condition."

"What's that?" asked Princess Gourmande.

"That I can eat from your plate and sleep in your bed for three nights," said the froggy voice which was really Grenwee in disguise.

"That's two conditions," said Gourmande. "But if you'll get my ball for me, I'll let you eat from my plate, and sleep in my bed as well."

The frog wondered whether there'd actually be room for anyone else in Gourmande's bed if Gourmande were in it. But even Grenwee had never been in the royal palace before, and if she could scare a princess, she reckoned nothing could stop her from being made Witch of the Year.

With ball in one hand and frog in the other, Princess Gourmande walked back to the palace. She stopped only to exchange a few words with the handsome young gardener, who had just planted a rose called 'Princess' in her honour.

"Thank you very much," said Gourmande. "But you should also plant a flower in honour of my little friend here."

"Certainly, Your Highness," said the gardener. "What about this purple flower?"

"Good," said Princess Gourmande. "What's it called?"

"Croakus," said the gardener.

That evening in the palace, the frog ate from the Princess's plate, and was also allowed to drink plenty of wine from the Princess's glass. When the meal ended, the frog was fat and sleepy and drunk.

"I'm going to bed," announced the Princess.

"An' hic arrk oopsh sho am I!" said the frog.

Within a few minutes, Grenwee was fast asleep. It was now time for Gourmande to carry out the most difficult part of her instructions. She felt under her pillow, took out her big sharp knife, and proceeded to cut off the frog's legs. Holding them in her hand, she ran down to the kitchen, where she dipped the legs in the milk, rolled them in flour and popped them in the frying pan with some butter and olive oil. After twelve minutes she added salt, pepper, lemon juice, parsley and chives, melted some more butter, chopped up the garlic, and poured the butter and garlic over the legs. Then do you know what she did? She closed her eyes, held her nose, and ate them.

"Actually," Gourmande told her father the next day, "they were rather nice. A little bit like chicken."

Grenwee never troubled anybody again. Not only was she unable to move, but she was also unable to change back into a witch. (If you think that's strange, see if *you* can change from a frog into a witch without using your legs.) She died soon afterwards, and the gardener buried her under the croakus. The King spread the happy news all over the kingdom, and the French people rejoiced to hear that their princess had rid them of the wicked witch.

As for the handsome gardener, he and Gourmande fell in love and so the King, without using any magic at all, turned him into a prince. They were married, and at their wedding feast Gourmande insisted that the main dish should be frogs' legs. From that day to this, the French have copied the example of their princess, and if you go into any good French restaurant you'll find that they're still serving frogs' legs cooked in butter, olive oil, and garlic.

The Ring and The Lamp

When Sultan Aladdin lay dying, he sent for his two sons, Ringading and Gongalong. The brothers were very similar in looks and character, but they were always jealous of each other and so they never stopped quarrelling. Aladdin was afraid that once he was dead, the brothers would fight for power and so cause great suffering to the people.

"Now, listen carefully," he said, as they stood on either side of his bed. "When I'm gone, you're to share everything equally between you. Ringading will rule over the eastern half of the country, and Gongalong over the western. You'll each have your own castle, you'll each take half my possessions, and you'll each mind your own business. Just one more thing: my grave is to be exactly halfway between east and west, and with me you're to bury this old ring and this old lamp. If either of you disobeys my orders, an eternal curse will fall on you."

The brothers agreed to do as they'd been told, whereupon Aladdin said, "Aaah!" and died.

He was buried between east and west, his possessions were divided equally between the brothers, and that should have been that. But it wasn't. Ringading kept wondering why his father had taken the ring and the lamp with him, and Gongalong kept wondering the same thing. Neither Aladdin nor his late wife, the Princess Badroulboudour, had ever told them the secret of the ring and the lamp, but the brothers wanted them simply because they'd been told they couldn't have them.

"They must be very special if father wanted to be buried with them," said Ringading to himself.

"If father wanted to be buried with them," said Gongalong to himself, "they must be very special."

One midnight, Ringading picked up his spade and set out for his father's grave. When he reached it, who should he see but Gongalong, standing on the other side of the grave, also carrying a spade.

"What are you doing here?" asked Ringading.

"The same as you," said Gongalong.

As each had caught the other, they could hardly blame one another, and so they agreed to dig up the grave together. They dug until they had uncovered their father's body, and the sight of this made them very afraid. They remembered Aladdin's curse, and almost expected him to leap out of the grave and chop their heads off. But he didn't — perhaps because dead bodies find it difficult to leap anywhere.

"The ring is on his eastern hand," said Ringading, "so it belongs to me."

"The lamp is in his western hand," said Gongalong, "so it belongs to me."

(A voice inside their heads said, "The ring and the lamp are in Aladdin's hands, so they belong to him.")

But in spite of the voice and in spite of their fear, they took the ring and the lamp, threw the earth back on top of their father, and ran home without even saying goodbye to each other.

Ringading could see nothing special at all about the ring, but as it was rather dirty after being in the earth, he decided to clean it up. And no sooner had he given it a rub than a huge and terrifying genie rose out of the earth and said:

"I am the slave of the ring. What can I do for you?"

"D . . . d . . . do for me?" asked Ringading.

"You are my master," said the genie. "I am yours to command."

"Really?" said Ringading. "That sounds interesting. What can you do?"

"Anything, master," said the genie, "so long as it isn't harmful."

"Could you kill my brother?" asked Ringading.

"Some people would say that was harmful," replied the genie.

"I wouldn't," said Ringading.

"He would," said the genie.

"All right," said Ringading. "Show me what my brother's doing at this moment."

"Easy," said the genie. He clapped his hands, and a screen appeared, right in the middle of the room. On this screen Ringading saw his brother, Gongalong, sitting in his living room watching a large screen on which Ringading sat in his living room watching a large screen on which . . . etc.

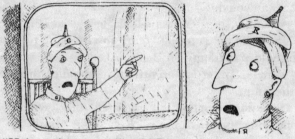

"He's spying on me!" said Ringading.

"That's right," said the genie. "And he's caught you spying on him."

"He can't do that!" complained Ringading.

"Oh, yes he can," replied the genie. "He's got the genie of the lamp to help him."

The same conversation was taking place between Gongalong and his genie, and from that hour on there was intense competition between the two brothers. Ringading built himself a castle with one hundred rooms. Gongalong built one with one hundred and ten. Ringading extended his to one hundred and twenty, so Gongalong extended his to two hundred. In the end they agreed to stick at a thousand each, but then they couldn't think what to do with a thousand rooms so they got the genies to shrink the castles back to one hundred.

"He's got me running round in circles," grumbled the genie of the ring.

"He's really getting on my wick," moaned the genie of the lamp.

Ringading decided he wanted fifty wives, so Gongalong married sixty. Ringading went up to seventy, Gongalong up to a hundred, and they finished with two hundred and fifty wives each. Then they decided that two hundred and fifty wives were too much trouble, so they agreed to settle on ten.

"Now, what are we supposed to do with all those extra wives?" moaned the genie of the ring.

"We'd better leave them in all those extra rooms," said the genie of the lamp.

The genies were kept busy night and day providing new buildings, new machines, and new entertainments. Soon the brothers were even racing each other to the moon and beyond. But in the meantime their people grew poorer and poorer, for the brothers never spared a thought for their suffering subjects.

"We can't go on," moaned the genie of the ring.

"But we can't go off," grumbled the genie of the lamp.

One day the thought occurred to Ringading that his brother might be planning to invade the east and become ruler over the whole country. At the very same moment it occurred to Gongalong that Ringading might be planning to invade the west. The brothers therefore summoned their genies, and each demanded an army so that they could defend themselves.

The genies then had the problem of deciding whether armies were harmful or not, and as this was much too difficult for them to solve on their own, they went together to the Ministry for Do's and Don'ts. Here they were greeted by a charming female genie with light brown hair, who took them to a colleague, who introduced them to an official, who passed them on to a higher official, who led them down the corridor and into the presence of the Minister himself.

"Don't be shy," said the Minister. "Do sit down. And do tell me what I can do for you, but don't worry if I don't do it."

MR. RODGERS.

They explained the problem to him, and he opened a drawer in his desk and consulted a list. Then he went to a filing-cabinet and consulted a file. Then he went to a shelf and consulted a catalogue. Then he motioned to the genies to go with him, and they all went off to a huge room which contained thousands and thousands of books. The Minister found a ladder, climbed (rather shakily) to the very top row of the books, pulled one out, climbed down (very shakily), blew off the dust, and opened it.

"Armies," he read. "See Section 42, sub-section 37, paragraph 16b."

He turned the pages.

"Armies," he read, "are not in themselves harmful. Whether an army is harmful or not will depend on the use made of it by the genie's master. If a master were to order a feather duster and then poke it in an enemy's eye, the genie could in no way be held responsible for the harmful effect. Similarly, the genie cannot be held responsible if a master makes harmful use of an army. Genies are therefore obliged to provide armies on request."

The genies thanked the Minister for his help.

"Don't mention it," said the Minister. "And do come again."

Off went the genies to provide Ringading and Gongalong with their armies. As soon as Ringading saw what a strong army he had, he set out to invade the west. At the same moment, Gongalong had set out with his army to invade the east. The two armies met exactly halfway between east and west, and in no time at all had completely wiped each other out. Only Ringading and Gongalong survived, and they stood facing each other across their father's grave.

"It was very wicked of you," said Ringading, "to steal our father's lamp."

"And it was very wicked of you," said Gongalong, "to steal our father's ring."

"His curse is on you," said Ringading.

"And on you," said Gongalong.

"I suggest," said Ringading, "that you put the lamp back in our father's grave."

"All right," said Gongalong, "if you put the ring back there as well."

So the brothers dug up their father's grave, and Ringading put the ring on his father's finger, and Gongalong put the lamp in his father's hand. But in fact Ringading had no intention of leaving the ring there. He pulled out his sword, and plunged it straight into Gongalong's heart. At the very same moment Gongalong, who had no intention of leaving the lamp there, plunged his sword straight into Ringading's heart. And the two brothers fell head-first into their father's grave and never moved again.

When the people heard that the wicked brothers were dead, they rejoiced. The grave was covered over again, and the brothers' eldest sons (who were much more sensible than their fathers) became joint rulers of the country. As for the ring and the lamp, they remained buried beneath the ground, while the genies were given jobs at the Ministry of Do's and Don'ts. The genie of the ring was put in charge of the Do's. He and the genie with the light brown hair fell in love and wanted to get married, so they did. The genie of the lamp was put in charge of the Don'ts. He didn't fall in love with anyone and didn't want to get married, so he didn't. But they both lived happily ever after.

DO'S   DON'TS

Uncle Willy's Brilliant Disguise

Hi, there! It's me again — Wolfie. I thought you'd like to hear Uncle Willy's story. What a story! What a genius! But if you read the history books, you'd think he was a fool. So stand by for the true story of the wolf in sheep's clothing.

Uncle Willy loved his lamb and mutton. Well, who doesn't? But as any wolf will tell you, mutton and lamb don't grow on trees. If you want them, you've got to catch them. You might think that's easy, since sheep are just bundles of wool tied together, and they'll do what they're told and go where they're pushed. But where there's sheep, there are shepherds, and shepherds are not good for wolves.

Your best chance is for your four-legged lunch to wander away from the flock, so that nobody sees the two of you get together. If you're spotted, there'll be such a bleaty panic that in no time the shepherd will have got his gun out and, BANG! One sheepless, lunchless, headless wolf.

Uncle Willy tried everything. He used to stand behind a tree and send out howls of invitation, but he never had an acceptance. He willed the sheep to come to him, but they wouldn't. He even tried calling for help once, but the only one to take any notice was the shepherd, so Uncle Willy didn't stay to be helped.

The solution to the problem came one glorious spring day when Uncle Willy found a dead sheep in a ditch. (Not a sheepskin, as the books will tell you. Sheep don't die and then undress themselves.) He spent hours nuzzling, biting and nibbling, and in the end he had just what he wanted — a complete sheep disguise from the silly black face to the stumpy white tail. With a good deal of wriggling, pulling and squeezing, he inserted himself into his new skin and went off to the nearest pond to have a look at his reflection. He nearly jumped into the water to gobble himself up. What a sheep! What a disguise! He had a meal-ticket for life.

With a tingle in his teeth and a tickle in his tongue, Uncle Willy headed hungrily for the sheep-field. (You may wonder why he didn't eat the body of the dead sheep. But if you found a chunk of meat in a ditch, would you eat it?) Heart thumping, he left the forest and wandered across the grass. Nobody took any notice. He pretended to do some nibbling, shook himself as sheep sometimes do, and even let out a little bleat or two. Nothing happened. He was a sheep among sheep. The shepherd, munching his cheese sandwiches under a tree, never so much as glanced at him.

It was time for a bit of conversation. Uncle Willy picked out a likely-looking lamb on the far side of the field from the shepherd.

"Hello!" baaed Uncle Willy.

"Hello!" baaed the lamb.

"My word," said Uncle Willy, "you *are* a little sweetie-pie!"

"What's a sweetie-pie?" asked the lamb.

"You are," said Uncle Willy. "Or you soon will be. So young, so tender! What a pity you're eating the wrong food."

"The wrong food?" echoed the lamb.

"Well, this grass is no good for you," said Uncle Willy. "It's much too green."

"Too green?" echoed the lamb.

"What you need," said Uncle Willy, "is pink grass."

"Pink grass?" echoed the lamb.

"Pink grass," repeated Uncle Willy. "Like you find in the woods."

"I've never seen pink grass," said the lamb.

"Not many lambs have," said Uncle Willy. "There isn't much of it about. But I know where to find it. Come with me, and we'll have a special treat."

The lamb wanted to ask its mummy first, but Uncle Willy said the pink grass was to be their little secret, and the lamb should forget about mummy and stick with good old Auntie. And so the two of them stole off to the woods, where Uncle Willy had his special treat and the lamb learned a lesson he would never be able to use.

Now this is where the history books start telling a load of lies. They say that Uncle Willy — merely called The Wolf, as if one wolf is the same as any other wolf — decided to spend the night in the sheep pen, so he could kill a fat sheep and gorge himself till breakfast time. But along came the shepherd to grab himself a sheep for *his* dinner, and the sheep that he grabbed was Uncle Willy. Some say this was coincidence, others that the shepherd recognized the wolf. But they all agree that Uncle Willy never left that pen alive, and it was his own fault for pretending to be what he wasn't.

"Pure fiction, old boy," says Uncle Willy, who's up here with me in Valhowla. "Absolute piffle!" (He talks like that — he's from the posher side of the family.) "If you'd eaten a whole lamb in the afternoon, would you want to eat a sheep in the night?"

I'd say that was as unlikely as me eating Red Riding Hood plus her fifteen-stone Granny.

"And why would I spend the night in the pen, eh?" asks Uncle Willy. "Start eating a sheep in the pen, and you'll get yourself crushed in the panic, what?"

Quite right. Not to mention having the shepherd come and find out what all the noise is for.

"All I had to do," says Uncle Willy, "was come to the field, get a sheep or lamb interested in my pink grass, and I was made for the rest of my days. I'd have been extremely stupid to get myself shut up in the pen!"

And Uncle Willy is not stupid. Uncle Willy is brilliant.

"And even if I had been in the pen, which I wasn't," says Uncle Willy, "would I have stood there and let the shepherd make mutton chops out of me?"

No, he wouldn't. Nobody could ever have made mutton chops out of Uncle Willy.

"All lies," says Uncle Willy. "Trying to make me look a fool, just because I made *them* look fools."

So what is the true story? How did brilliant Uncle Willy really die?

"Darn bad luck, old boy," says Uncle Willy. "Nothing but darn bad luck."

I'd better tell the rest of the story myself. Uncle Willy gets upset just thinking about it. By the time he'd finished the lamb, it was already getting dark, and he set off for home at a very slow, digesting pace. He was in no hurry anyway, and it was good fun just thinking about the lifetime of easy meat that lay ahead of him.

As he burped his way contentedly through the shadows of the forest, his progress was being watched by a dozen pairs of wolf-eyes. And what the wolf-eyes saw was not Uncle Willy burping his way contentedly through the forest. What they saw was one very fat, very isolated sheep with 'supper' written all over it.

Uncle Willy saw them only at the very last moment.

"Hold on, chaps," he cried. "I'm not a sheep! I'm a wolf!"

This did have the effect of stopping the leader of the pack, who became helpless with laughter and simply rolled around, shrieking, "He says he's a wolf! A sheep pretending to be a wolf!" But unfortunately the rest of the pack didn't share his sense of humour, and what they did to Uncle Willy was certainly no laughing matter. By the time they'd found out that Uncle Willy really was a wolf, Uncle Willy was no longer a wolf. There were a few mumbled apologies, which fell on dead ears, and then they all sloped off feeling — if the word isn't too inappropriate — rather sheepish.

It was the shepherd who found the remains of the lamb and the remains of Uncle Willy in the remains of the sheepskin. I suppose he was just like Granny and Red Riding Hood: crazy to get himself on the front page of the newspapers. So he made up the version that's gone down in history, *Clever Shepherd Outsmarts Wolf*. Only it takes a wolf to outsmart a wolf.

I did point out to Uncle Willy that the official moral could still apply, though: don't pretend to be what you're not. But Uncle Willy just growled and said the shepherd hadn't done too badly out of it.

"Besides, old boy," said Uncle Willy, "I was just darned unlucky. How often do you expect a wolf to be taken for a sheep?"

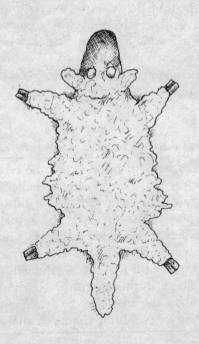

44

The Biggest Shock in Athletics History

ZZZZ

Even now it's hard to believe, but the record books show that it's a fact: Terry Tortoise challenged Harry Hare to a race, and beat him. How did it happen? Aesop's History of the A.A.A.*** says that the hare was over-confident, lay down for a nap, and woke up too late to catch the tortoise. But why did Terry challenge Harry in the first place? And why did Harry come over sleepy during the race? Newly discovered documents show the answer to be a tale of crime and deceit that will for ever bring shame on all tortoises.

*** A.A.A. = Animal Athletics Association

Terry was slow-moving, slow-talking, and fast-spending. He was a gambler and a playboy, mixing with all the wrong animals, and the despair of his family and friends. When he reached his fiftieth birthday he gave the biggest party anyone could remember, but his guests included the worst criminals in the forest: Killa the Gorilla, Rip-Off the Tiger, Fingers Fox and The Thieving Magpie. By the time the party was over, there was not a single honest guest that hadn't been beaten, mugged or pick-pocketed.

"Grrreat parrrty, Terrrry!" said Rip-Off the Tiger as he departed. "I got morrre happy rrreturrrns on your birrrthday than I get on my own."

"Super party, Terry," said Killa the Gorilla. "We made monkeys out of everybody!"

But the good life costs money, and the time soon came when Terry was shell over heels in debt. All the animals were demanding payment, and as it was no use him running away (even if he'd had a three-day start, they'd have caught him in twenty minutes), he had no choice but to face them. His usual trick was to curl up inside his shell and pretend to be asleep, but that's not so easy when there's an elephant knocking at your door — or a swarm of ants crawling under it. Terry was in trouble, and only a miracle could save him.

It was when Harry Hare won the gold medal in the Three A's cross-forest open race that Terry had his great idea. While the crowd was still cheering, he plodded across the grass till he stood just in front of Harry, looked up at him, and said in his loudest voice, "Call yourself . . . erm . . . a runner?"

"I beg your pardon?" asked Harry.

"If you're . . . erm . . . a runner," said Terry, "then I'm . . . erm . . . a streak of lightning."

Harry laughed, and so did all the other animals.

"You can laugh," said Terry, "but . . . erm . . . a good tortoise'll beat a good hare any day — and . . . erm . . . you're not even a good hare!"

"I've just won the gold medal," said Harry, who could scarcely believe his long ears.

"Only because I wasn't . . . erm . . . in the race," said Terry.

"Don't be silly, Terry," said Harry. "I could beat you with all four legs tied together."

"Anyone could beat me," said Terry, "if . . . erm . . . I had all four legs tied together."

"Not yours," said Harry. "Mine!"

"I'll bet you . . . erm . . . a hundred thousand pounds," said Terry, "that I can beat you in a race."

"You haven't got a hundred thousand pounds," said Harry.

"If you win," said Terry, "I'll . . . erm . . . sell my shell to pay you."

This brought gasps of astonishment from Harry and the rest of the animals, because a tortoiseshell is very valuable. Harry himself didn't have a hundred thousand pounds, but as all the animals wanted to bet on this race, the money was soon raised. A millionaire dormouse agreed to buy the shell if Terry lost, and if he won, then he would get the hundred thousand pounds. Bookie the Bear and Squooge the Squirrel took charge of the money (Bookie was strong enough to guard it, and Squooge was educated enough to count it), but everyone agreed that Terry should look after his own shell until he'd lost the race.

"After all," said Harry," he could hardly run away with it!"

The race was to take place the following Saturday, which gave them a week to prepare. Harry did his usual training exercises, with sprints and jogs and canters, while Terry slowly made his way to the hide-out of one of his criminal friends, Hoodlum the Hedgehog.

"Ullo, Terry," said Hoodlum. "What's this I 'ear about you 'avin' a race wiv 'Arry?"

"So you know already," said Terry. "News travels . . . erm . . . fast."

"No," said Hoodlum. "It's you wot travels slow. Wotcher plannin' then?"

"When I win," said Terry, "it'll be my big . . . erm . . . pay-off."

"An' 'ow are you 'opin' ter beat 'Arry?" scoffed Hoodlum. "'E'll be 'ome before you got yer 'ind legs over the startin' line!"

"Not if you . . . erm . . . help me," said Terry.

Hoodlum didn't see how he or anyone else could help Terry beat the champion, but Terry said it was all connected with winter.

"Wotcher mean?" asked Hoodlum.

"It's what you hedgehogs . . . erm . . . *do* in winter," said Terry.

"We don't do nuffin'!" said Hoodlum. "We sleep."

"Exactly," said Terry. "And what . . . erm . . . makes you sleep?"

"That's my business," said Hoodlum.

"Well," said Terry, "it's . . . erm . . . a bit of your business that I'm . . . erm . . . after."

There was a slight pause as Hoodlum looked shiftily round the clearing in which they were standing. Then he sidled up close to Terry, and speaking very quietly out of the corner of his mouth said:

"You want some stuff, do yer?"

"Enough . . . erm . . . sleeping powders . . ."

"Sh! Not so loud!"

The conversation continued in whispers. Most of it seemed to be about a cake. Hoodlum said Terry's plan took the cake, Terry said the race would be a piece of cake, and Hoodlum said he wanted more of the cake. Then they quarrelled about how much of the cake each should have, but finally they agreed, and Terry began the long trudge home, with half-a-dozen sleeping powders tucked under his shell.

When Saturday came, the animals turned out in great numbers to cheer their champion home, and there was loud laughter when Terry staggered to the starting line.

"Well, at least you'll be second, Terry!" shouted Killa the Gorilla.

"No, he'll arrrrive firrrrst," said Rip-Off the Tiger. "Firrrrst of Januarrrry next yearrrr."

The millionaire dormouse took his place, carrying a large placard which said, "Go well, go shell."

"Look," said Harry, who was really a kind-hearted hare, "I don't like to see anybody homeless. Why don't we call it off?"

"Scared, eh?" said Terry.

"You know you can't beat me!" said Harry.

"You're much too . . . erm . . . sure of yourself," shouted Terry in his loudest voice. "Next you'll be saying you could . . . erm . . . sleep all afternoon and still . . . erm . . . beat me."

"And so I could," said Harry.

"Well," said Terry, "let's . . . erm . . . drink to a good race. And may the better . . . erm . . . tortoise win."

So saying, he produced two gourds of nectar, one of which he handed to Harry. It was the one with Hoodlum's powder in it.

"Good health to you, then!" said Harry.

"And sweet dreams to you!" said Terry.

The rest of the story is common knowledge. Harry raced away into a big lead, came over sleepy, lay down, and didn't wake up until it was too late. The animals were all furious, and Harry — who never knew how he had been tricked — went quite crazy with grief and shame. He vowed that he would never run again, and indeed it may well be Harry who gave rise to the saying, 'as mad as a March hare'.

As for Terry, he paid his debts and cheated his way into the record books, but in the end his crime didn't pay. He had a violent quarrel with Hoodlum the Hedgehog, who was not happy with his slice of the cake, and they were both found dead three days later in the middle of a clearing. Terry lay on his back, with a hedgehog spine through his heart, and Hoodlum lay squashed under Terry.

"They must have bumped into each other," said Killa the Gorilla.

"Orrrr bumped each otherrrr off!" replied Rip-Off the Tiger.

The Beast

Most people know the story of how the ugly Prince became handsome (read *Beauty and the Beast*). Well, this is the story of how the handsome Prince became ugly before he became handsome.

The handsome Prince lived in a castle in the centre of town. He had mirrors everywhere so that he could admire himself coming and going, though sometimes he got so lost in admiration that he didn't know whether he was coming *or* going. He would spend hours gazing into his own fascinated eyes and making the servants polish the mirrors so that his reflection could be even more dazzling. But his favourite occupation was riding through the town in his golden coach, for the people would all bow to him as he went past. The old ladies would gasp, and the young ladies would swoon because he was so handsome. Of course, he would look straight ahead and pretend not to notice them.

The question on everybody's lips was, naturally, who would the Prince marry? Every girl in the land wanted to be his wife, and every mother in the land wanted to be his mother-in-law, but the Prince was in no hurry to find himself either a wife or a mother-in-law since he found so much pleasure in simply sharing his life with himself. Then one day he had a visit from the King and Queen (who lived in a different town).

"Now look here, my boy," said the King, "your mother and I feel . . . um . . . ah . . . well . . ."

"It's time you got married," said the Queen.

"Exactly," said the King.

"Every man in our family has a wife," said the Queen.

"I'm afraid that's true," said the King.

"And it's time you had one as well," said the Queen.

"Your time has come," said the King.

"But I don't want a wife!" cried the Prince.

"Nonsense!" said the Queen. "No man can be happy without a wife. Look at your father. Where would he be without me?"

"Don't answer that question," said the King, "but start looking for a bride."

"And let us know when you've found her," said the Queen, "because I shall want to organize the wedding."

Off went the King and Queen, and since their word was law (at least, the Queen's word was — even for the King), the Prince let it be known that he was looking for a bride. The news echoed round the country like a bell in a church, and in no time at all there were huge queues of girls at the castle gates, round the castle walls, down the castle driveway, and out into the town. There were girls of all sorts, shapes, sizes, colours — some with their mothers, some with their fathers, and even one or two with their husbands.

The Prince sat in the castle, and the girls were made to file past him. They were not allowed to speak because the Prince had made up his mind that he would not marry anyone who wasn't as beautiful as he was, and that was something he could judge with his eyes and not his ears.

He sat there hour after hour, murmuring, "Ugly, very ugly, hideous, vile, monstrous . . ." and every few minutes he would glance at the mirror to give himself some relief. Why look outside to find perfection when you can find it in your own reflection?

The girls would go back to their mothers, fathers, husbands and so on and report the Prince's verdict. Then they would either slink off home, or have their hair restyled and join the end of the queue again. Meanwhile, more and more girls were arriving. Prince-hunting had become the national sport, and the line of brides grew longer and longer, while the Prince's patience grew shorter and shorter.

"The trouble with my parents," he grumbled, "is that they've *always* been married. They just don't know what life is all about."

And after four days of non-stop bride inspections and rejections, the Prince was actually thinking of disobeying the King and Queen when . . .

He shook his head and rubbed his eyes three times. Was he dreaming, or was she real? Golden hair as soft as down, eyes shining like mirrors, marble-smooth skin, cherry-sweet lips . . . She was, without doubt, the most beautiful thing he had seen since he had last glanced at his reflection. He stood up, and smiled the smile that had launched ten thousand dreams.

"She's the one!' he cried. "I'm going to marry her. Tell all the others to go away."

The servants hurried off to tell the waiting crowds that the Prince had found his bride. The news was greeted with much mumbling and grumbling: "Been waiting for days . . . travelled miles . . . took a week off work . . . it's a fix . . . what about the semi-finals and finals?"

Gradually the people dispersed, while inside the castle the Prince took his bride-to-be into his own favourite hall of mirrors.

"Now then," he said, "let's have a good look at the two of us. My word, you really are almost as gorgeous as me. What's your name, future Princess?"

But the girl didn't answer. Instead, she lifted her hand, and in one swift movement pulled off her hair and face and threw them on the floor. (They were really a wig and a mask.) The creature the Prince now found before him was the ugliest he had ever seen: its head was as bald as a vulture's, its skin was covered with toad-warts, its eyes were piggy, its nose beaky, and its mouth fishy. Its ears stuck up like fox ears, and its cheeks hung down like cow udders. It may have had a human body, but its face was positively beastly. The Prince was so shocked that he couldn't even keep his eyes on himself.

"My name," said the creature in a voice like that of a hoarse crow, "is Mrs Sweet. Two days ago you told my daughter, Sugar, that she was yucky, and she's been crying ever since. So now you'll find out for yourself what it's like to be yucky."

The witch — for that was what she was — made some strange movements with her hands, and cried out:

"From south to north, from west to east,
There'll never be an uglier beast!"

Then she picked up her wig and mask and put them on again. "Have a good look at yourself in the mirror," she said, "because that's how you'll stay till someone agrees to marry you."

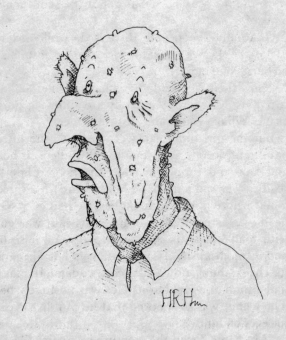

60

Cackling like a hen that's laid a golden egg, Mrs Sweet turned her back on her fiancé, or rather her ex-fiancé, and walked away from Prince and castle. And when the Prince at last dared to look into the mirror, the face that he saw was the face of Mrs Sweet.

He went out into the corridor, where two guards stood before the door.

"Yaaark!" screamed the first guard, and "Uggle!" gulped the second. Without exchanging a word, they each decided immediately that a guard's first duty was to guard himself. They had completed their goodbyes before the Prince could even say hullo.

It was the same with everyone he met. One glimpse was enough to send soldiers and servants racing for the nearest door or window, and soon there was only one person left in the castle — though even he wasn't sure if he was a person or not.

MAD BEAST LOOSE IN CASTLE ran the newspaper headline, and an authoritative source (Fred Nutter, palace guard) was quoted as saying that the Beast had eaten both the Prince and his bride-to-be. "It were 'orrible," said the source, "an' someone'll 'ave ter do somethin' about it. Only it won't be me."

When at last the Prince plucked up the courage to come out of the castle, he found the streets deserted, and all doors and windows bolted and barred. Occasionally he would catch sight of people in the distance, but they would also catch sight of him, and nobody stayed to take a closer look. He tried banging on doors and shouting out that he was the Prince.

"Talk about the wolf in sheep's clothing!" said a voice from behind the shutters.

"No, he's not," said another voice. "He's the wolf in wolf's clothing!"

"I'm not a wolf!" cried the Prince. "I'm the Prince!"

But nobody believed him.

"I'll marry anyone who agrees to marry me," he shouted.

But nobody did.

"I hate you all!" he wailed.

"And we hate you!" called voices from behind shutters.

Life as a Beast was beastly.

The Prince wandered sadly into the park, where birds squawked and flew to the tops of trees, animals cowered behind bushes, and ducks dived headfirst into the lake and paddled away.

"Not even a duck would marry me now!" groaned the Prince. (Though it's doubtful whether a duck would have married him even before he became a Beast.)

Beside the lake there was a bench, and sitting on the bench was a man. The Prince walked a little nearer, expecting the man to jump up and run away, but the man did not move.

"Hullo," said the Prince.

"Hullo," said the man.

Now the Prince saw that the man was dressed in rags.

"Not many people about," said the Prince.

"No," said the man, "they're all afraid of the Beast. I was surprised to hear you coming."

The Prince saw that the man was blind.

"You're the first person I've spoken to for days," he said, and suddenly felt tears running down his cheeks.

"You're a stranger here, are you?" asked the blind man.

"No," said the Prince. "I'm the Beast."

"Oh!" said the blind man. "Well, I think it's time I was going . . ."

"Please don't go!" begged the Prince. "You see, I'm not really a beast at all. Underneath, I'm a handsome prince."

"Handsome prince, eh?" said the blind man. "Well, you don't sound like a beast, I must say. More like a lunatic."

"I'm not a lunatic!" cried the Prince. "I'm the Prince."

He then told the blind man his whole story from start to finish, ending with the fact that he would have to stay a beast until someone agreed to marry him.

"Lucky you!" said the blind man.

"What's lucky about me?" asked the Prince.

"I shall be ugly and blind for the rest of my life," said the blind man. "At least you have something to hope for."

"What hope is there of anyone ever loving me?" asked the Prince.

"Well," said the blind man, "if I met a lady who was kind to me, I expect I'd love her however ugly she was. It's not everyone that sees with their eyes, you know. One day you could meet a lady that'll see you with her heart."

"Does such a person exist?" asked the Prince.

"Oh, yes," said the blind man. "I'd marry you myself, only I'd look silly in a dress."

The Prince laughed for the first time since he'd become a Beast.

"I'm going away from the town now," he said. "I can't go on living here. But I've got another castle deep in the forest, where I shall hide myself away. Will you come and live with me there?"

The blind man was delighted to accept the invitation, and the Prince led him to the forest, where they lived together for four years. The Beast saw to everything the blind man couldn't do, and the blind man cheered the Beast up by making him laugh and giving him hope. But then, one dark winter's day, the blind man caught cold and died. The Beast wept bitterly, and he buried his friend in the garden, with beautiful bushes of red roses to mark the spot where the blind man lay.

Not long afterwards, Beauty's father rode into the forest, plucked one of the red roses, and . . . the rest of the story you already know. But you should also be told that a few years after the Prince and Beauty were married, they became King and Queen. And they proved to be the wisest and kindest King and Queen the country had ever known.

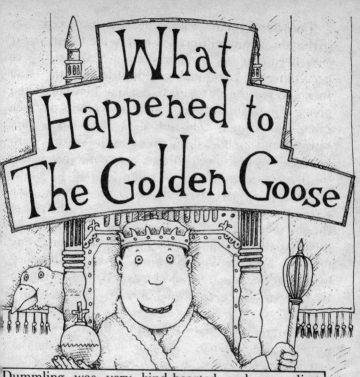

What Happened to The Golden Goose

Dummling was very kind-hearted and very dim-witted. One day he shared his lunch with a little old man, and as a reward was given a goose with golden feathers. When some people tried to steal the feathers, they got stuck to one another, and Dummling walked into town not noticing the line of stuck-together people behind him. The sight was so funny that Princess Mona burst out laughing. As Princess Mona had never laughed before, the King was so pleased that he gave her hand in marriage to Dummling, who thus became heir to the throne. You may think that this was not the cleverest way to find a future king, and you would be right.

When the King died, Dummling decided to have a party. Mona thought this was killingly funny, as she'd expected a funeral. And she simply collapsed with laughter when Dummling said he was inviting every citizen to the party. (You may wonder why this was so funny, but you must understand that Princess Mona had a very peculiar sense of humour. After all, what's so funny about a line of people stuck together?)

Dummling sent messengers all over the country to invite everyone to the party. Unfortunately, he forgot to tell them when, so nobody came. After Dummling and Mona had waited in vain for two weeks, Dummling sent the messengers out again to announce that the party would be on Saturday.

At first light on Saturday, the castle was invaded by thousands of people, and by breakfast time there wasn't a single crumb of food in the whole Palace. By lunchtime there wasn't a single item of furniture, and King Dummling stood at the door in his pink-and-white striped underpants apologizing to people that he had nothing left to give them. Queen Mona, in her bra and knickers, was helpless with laughter on her throne.

At three p.m. when there was no longer any glass in the windows or paper on the walls, King Dummling heard a loud noise in the garden. He and Queen Mona rushed out, and found a long line of people stuck together, following a man with a stubbly chin who was holding the golden goose. This was too much for Queen Mona, who shrieked with laughter, and lay flat on her back kicking her legs in the air.

"What a spendid game," said King Dummling. "Can I play, too?"

"It's not a game, Your Majesty," said the stubble-chinned man. "We can't seem to let go."

"Can't let go?" said King Dummling. "That's funny."

"Hilarious!" squealed Queen Mona, and rolled helplessly into the duck pond.

"What's happened, then?" asked King Dummling.

"Well, it's like this, Your Majesty," said Stubble-Chin. "We're all very poor, you see. Especially me. I've a wife and six children to feed, but the only way I could earn enough money is to work, and unfortunately — through no fault of my own — I don't like work. Work always makes me tired, you see. So I came to your party hoping you might help me, seeing that I'm so poor and hungry. But as I couldn't get out of bed till late, everything had gone before I got here. Then I spotted this here goose, and thought I'd borrow a feather or two, just enough to feed my little ones. But I got stuck. And these people had the same idea as me, and they got stuck as well."

"What a sad story," said King Dummling. "Of course I'll help you."

So saying, he took the goose out of Stubble-Chin's hands. This at once removed the stickiness, and as everybody had been pulling hard to get away from his neighbour, the result was a long line of people falling, just like a line of dominoes. Queen Mona, who had been clambering out of the duck pond, simply fell straight back in again.

"Now," said King Dummling, "how many of you people are poor?"

"All of us," said all of them.

"Then I'd better give all of you a feather," said the King.

"Hurray!" said the crowd, and everybody rushed at the King, who fell over with the goose on top of him, and ten men on top of the goose. The men naturally got stuck again, and so did the other men who tried to pull the ten men off the goose. Queen Mona saw all this from the duck pond and nearly split her sides quacking.

"Perhaps you could all just stand in a line," gasped King Dummling, but nobody took any notice.

"Stand in a line!" shouted Stubble-Chin in a very loud voice, and everybody stood in a line.

"Right, Your Majesty," said Stubble-Chin, who was first in the line, "you can give us the feathers. Especially me."

Dummling got up, brushed the footprints off his tummy, tucked the goose under one arm, and pulled out a golden feather.

"Ouch!" said the goose.

"Thank you, Your Majesty," said Stubble-Chin.

"Hurray!" said the crowd.

Dummling walked along the line, handing out golden feathers, but the line never seemed to get any shorter.

"Haven't you had a feather already?" he asked a bushy-bearded man.

"No, Your Majesty," said the man. "Not one." (It was true. He hadn't had one. He'd had three.)

On went the King, until at last there was nothing left on the goose but a bodyful of goose pimples. The crowd sighed and booed and went away, Queen Mona crawled out of the duck pond, and together she and King Dummling walked back to the palace. By now there was nobody left — even the ministers, counsellors, servants and guards had gone.

"I do like being King," said Dummling.

Mona howled with laughter. (Why? Could it have been Dummling's pink-and-white striped underpants?)

What Dummling and Mona didn't know was that at that very moment the man with the stubbly chin was walking round the town with a crown on his head and ten gold feathers in his pocket, telling everyone that *he* was King. And he said it in such a loud voice that everybody believed him. He marched up to the palace with a great crowd of ministers, counsellors, servants and guards behind him, then he knocked loudly on the door. Dummling opened it, and the man with the stubbly chin said:

"Who are you?"

"I'm King Dummling," said King Dummling.

"Nonsense," said Stubble-Chin. "Kings don't wear pink-and-white striped underpants. Kings wear crowns. And who's wearing a crown?"

"You are," said the King.

"That's right," said Stubble-Chin. "Off with his head."

And before Dummling even knew that his head was on, it was off. When Mona saw Dummling's head rolling over the floor, while his body stood pink-and-white at the door, she hooted like a tickled owl.

"Who are you?" asked Stubble-Chin.

"Whooo whooo whooo . . . the Queen . . . whooo whooo!" said the Queen.

"Nonsense," said Stubble-Chin. "Queens sit on thrones. They don't stand hooting in their undies. Off with her head."

Queen Mona's head went giggling across the floor, and there was a loud cheer from the crowd. Stubble-Chin sent the servants round to make a collection for the new King.

Stubble-Chin reigned for fifty years, and by the time he died, he was the richest king the country had ever known.

As for the golden goose, it caught its death of cold the day after the party. A clever scientist found the body, and spent a long time studying it, in the hope that he might find out how to make gold. He, too, became a very rich man. He never learned how to make gold, but he did learn how to make the stickiest glue in the world.

Crying Wolf, Laughing Wolf

Men are clever. They feed their sheep, and protect them against the big bad wolf, so the poor suckers believe that man is really their best friend. Even when the farmer comes along with the knife in his hand, they probably think he wants to scratch their backs for them. What other animal can have three meals a day, and keeps his meals sitting in the back garden waiting to be eaten? But if poor old Wolfie comes along and gets one meal in a month, he'll be accused of trespass, theft, murder — every crime in the book. "See what an evil creature the wolf is!" the shepherd tells his flock. "That's right," say all the little dumb-heads. "Aren't we lucky to have men to protect us!"

But every so often, one of us outsmarts those clever humans. Uncle Willy did it with his sheepskin overcoat, but then Uncle Willy had his bit of bad luck. Another wolf of genius also outsmarted them, and actually lived to tell the tale. If I wasn't so modest, I'd tell you that the wolf of genius was me.

It all began when I discovered this hollow tree. Maybe you can't see a connection between a hollow tree and a free bite at the mutton, but maybe you're not as smart as me. It was in a clump on a hill overlooking the sheep-field, and it was big enough for me to hide in. Now, if you're thinking that I hid there waiting for a passing stray, forget it. By the time a stray passed that way, you'd have had a hollow dead tree containing a hollow dead wolf. No, dinners never come that easy.

This particular flock of sheep was guarded by a little boy. Little boys don't carry guns, and so at first I reckoned I was on to a good thing. (This was before I found the tree.) I went straight for the flock, they made their usual anti-wolf noises, the boy spotted me, and at the top of his voice he yelled, "Wolf! Wolf!" Before I could get even a lick of lamb, some men came running through the hedge on the far side and there were bullets whistling round my ears. I went back up that hill twice as fast as I'd come down it, and my heart thumped so hard I kept looking round to see who was kicking me.

Two days later I discovered the hollow tree. I was just nosing round the clump, wondering if I might find a dead sheep and do an Uncle Willy, when I nosed my way straight into this dark hole. "What a hiding-place!" I said to myself, and there and then I knew how to get my supper. Amazing! One moment the menu card was a total blank, and the next I had all my taste-buds practically bursting into flower.

Timing — that was the only tricky bit. If I didn't get the timing right, I could lose the sheep and a lot more besides. I had to be spotted before I was too far down the hill, and that wouldn't be easy, since sheep are pretty slow at spotting anything. My best chance was to act as stupid as them. So I came bounding out of the trees, howling, "Look out! I'm coming to get you!" There was immediate panic, and up jumped the boy with a loud cry of "Wolf! Wolf!" Yours truly did a quick about-turn and raced straight back up the hill, into the clump, and into the hollow tree.

The vital question was, had I disappeared before the men got to the field? If I hadn't, I was in trouble. If I had, someone else would be in trouble. My heart started rib-kicking again as the sound of men's voices drew nearer, but it did a little skip of joy when a child's voice said, "He ran into these trees." If the boy had to tell them where I'd gone, they couldn't have seen me for themselves.

"No sign of him," said a gruff voice not ten feet from the tip of my nose.

"Must've gone off into the woods," said another.

"Expect we've scared him off," said a third. "Well done, Johnny. You keep a good watch now."

Footsteps and voices faded into the distance again, but I sat very still in my hollow tree. I didn't even allow myself to chuckle.

I gave them plenty of time to go back to where they'd come from, then out I sneaked, tip-toed to the edge of the clump, and peeped out from behind a bush. Everything was back to normal: sheep grazing peacefully, boy under tree, no sign of big bad men.

"Here we go, then," I said to myself. "Round two." And down I raced.

"Look out, you stupid sheep, I'm coming to get you!"

Bleat, baaa, wolf, baaa, bleat! Wool flying in all directions. Up jumps the boy. "Wolf! Wolf!" he cries.

At top speed I race back up the hill, into the clump, and into the hollow tree.

Then it's the same story as before — footsteps and voices . . . closer and closer.

"I did!" says the little boy. "I did see him! He ran into these trees."

"He's not here," says one voice.

"No sign," says another.

"You sure you saw him?" asks a third.

"Yes," says the little boy. "He came down the hill, and then he ran back up again."

"Funny business," says the first voice.

"He must've moved pretty quick," says the second.

"Well, keep watch, Johnny," says the third. "But don't call out unless you're sure it's a wolf."

"It *is* a wolf!" says the boy.

Quite right, sonny, says I, and a mighty clever wolf at that! But of course I don't say it out loud. I just sit there, very still and very quiet, while they all go away.

Twice more I went down and up the hill, and twice more the boy shouted "Wolf! Wolf!" and the men came looking for me. Poor Johnny! If he hadn't been human, I could almost have felt sorry for him. You should have heard the way those men yelled at him after their fourth hunt for the where-wolf!

"If this is your idea of a joke . . ." one of them shouted.

"It's not a joke!" whined Johnny.

"Four times I've been up an' down this blessed hill," grumbled another.

"What you need, my lad," said a third, "is either a pair o' glasses or a good hiding."

Then the boy started crying, and one of the men thought he was laughing so he gave him a clip round the ear.

"That'll teach you," he shouted.

And soon, I said to myself, I shall teach *you*.

But you can't be too careful. I made one more trial run. Nobody came. They'd given up.

I peeped out from behind my bush, and looked down on my dinner.

"Yum, yum, and here I come!" I said, and set off down the hill. Even when I was close to them, the sheep didn't take any notice. They obviously expected me to turn round and chase back up the hill. As for the boy, he saw me all right, but he didn't know whether to shout "Wolf! Wolf!" or not, and in the end he let out a sort of "Woo! Woo!" sound — more like an owl than a howl.

I picked out the juiciest sheep I could find, and by the time I'd finished, the boy had taken the rest of the

flock home. Actually it was lucky for me that nobody did come, because I certainly couldn't have got back up the hill again that night, let alone fitted into the hollow tree.

Of course, this isn't the story you'll find in the history books. According to them, Johnny was telling lies all the time, and it was just sheer coincidence that eventually old Wolfie happened to come along.

"There you are," they say. "That proves that liars won't be believed when they tell the truth."

As I said before, they're clever. They're so clever that they don't even know when they've been outsmarted.

How Not to be a Giant Killer

ck's big mistake was to try to make a comeback.
aving retired as undefeated giant-killing champion
Cornwall, he should have left it at that. After all,
'd married the Duke's daughter, and one day he
buld be Duke himself. No worries about money,
busing, unemployment — Jack had it made. But once
fighter, always a fighter. He started longing for the
ight lights, the publicity, the razzamatazz of the
ant-killing game, and at last he could stand it no
nger and informed his wife that he was going out to
l a giant.

"Ts!" tutted Charlotte. "Just when I've put the dinner on!"

"I can't help that," said Jack. "A man's gotta do what a man's gotta do."

"Anyway," said Charlotte, "I thought you'd killed off all the giants already."

"In Cornwall I have," said Jack. "But there must be plenty left in Devon."

"Who wants to go to Devon?" snorted Charlotte.

"I do," said Jack. "To kill a giant."

And off he went to look for his horse, his sword and his cloak. You may remember that a grateful wizard had given Jack a horse that could run like the wind, a sword that could cut through anything, and a cloak that made its wearer invisible. The horse was out in the field grazing, as it had been doing for the last three years. When Jack climbed on its back and said "Giddy up!" the horse took one heavy step forward and its tummy bumped the ground.

"Can you still run like the wind?" asked Jack.

"I can't run at all," replied the horse. "Though I do have plenty of wind."

"Ah, well," said Jack, "I'll just have to walk. The exercise'll do me good."

Next, he searched for his sword, which he found in the garden shed under the lawn-mower. It had gone rusty. When Jack tried to cut the head off a dandelion with it, the blade snapped and fell off the handle.

"Ah, well," said Jack, "I'll just have to use my brains and my invisible cloak."

But he couldn't see his invisible cloak anywhere.

"It must have disappeared," said Jack. "Ah, well, I'll just have to move so fast that they can't see me. I'm off now, dear."

"Well, try and get back for dinner," said Charlotte.

Devon had only been three or four inches away on the map, but by dinner-time Jack was still in Cornwall and was feeling tired and hungry. He knocked on a nearby door, and a man opened it.

"Hullo," said Jack. "I'm Jack the Giant-Killer."

"And I'm the Duke of Cornwall," said the man, and shut the door in Jack's face.

The man in the next house said he was the King's grandfather, and the people in the third house had a little dog with giant-killing ideas of its own. Jack was

lucky to escape with nothing worse than a torn
trouser-seat. He gave up knocking on doors, and
walked sadly on with aching feet, a rumbling tum, and
a cold bottom. He walked all through the night until at
last he came to a sign which said, *Welcome to Devon.*

"Some welcome!" said Jack, and flopped down
exhausted at the side of the road and went to sleep.

As he slept, Jack dreamt that he was still knocking
on people's doors, and he kept calling out: "I'm Jack
the Giant-Killer! I'm the Duke's son-in-law!" But
nobody believed him in his dream either.

The next morning, two Devon giants named Klottid
and Kreem happened to come along the road. Just as
they drew close to Jack, he cried out, "I'm Jack the
Giant-Killer! I'm the Duke's son-in-law!"

"I've heard of him," said Klottid. "He killed all the
giants in Cornwall."

"In that case," said Kreem, "we'd better stop him
from killing all the giants in Devon."

When Jack finally woke up, he knew that he must be
very ill, because he couldn't move a muscle.

"Help! Help!" he cried. "I'm paralysed! Call the
doctor!"

There were two gigantic laughs and Jack, who was bound hand and foot (and everywhere else), was just able to turn his head enough to see the smiling faces of Klottid and Kreem.

"Jack the Giant-Killer, are you?" said Klottid.

"That's right," said Jack. "And I'm very ill . . . I'm . . ."

"Oh, dearie, dearie me," said Kreem. "Now which of us are you going to kill first?"

Jack suddenly realized that he was the prisoner of two giants.

"Oh!" he said. "Ah! Um! Well . . . no . . . look . . . I've retired! That's it . . . I've retired from killing giants."

"Ooh, thank Heavens for that!" said Klottid.

"What a relief!" said Kreem.

"So you've got nothing to be afraid of," said Jack.

"Ooh, what a relief!" said Klottid.

"Thank Heavens for that!" said Kreem.

"Mind you, Kreemy," said Klottid, "I knew he was *bound* to leave us alone!"

"Oh, so did I, Klotty," said Kreem. "He's much too tied up to bother about us!"

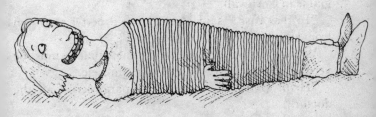

"So you can let me go," said Jack, "and I'll be on my way."

"What a sense of humour!" said Klottid.

"All those Cornish giants must have died laughing!" said Kreem.

Then they put poor tied-up Jack in a box (thus making him the very first Jack-in-the-Box) and invited all their friends to come and see. In those days there weren't very many giant-killers in captivity, and so before long giants were coming from all over the country (except Cornwall) to look and laugh. Klottid and Kreem charged them an entrance fee, and also served delicious teas in their front parlour. (Klottid Kreem Teas are still a tradition in Devon today.) There were soon Jack-the-Giant-Killer mugs and plates and T-shirts, *A History of Jack's Capture* — written by the famous historian, Liza Plenty — and a do-it-yourself Giant-Killer-Capture-Kit, which consisted of a signed picture of Klottid and Kreem, plus a piece of string. Business boomed, and everyone was happy. Everyone, that is, except Jack.

Day after day, week after week, Jack lay in his box thinking up escape plans. His first idea was to threaten the giants.

"If you don't let me go," he warned them, "you'll be in a lot of trouble."

"What sort of trouble?" asked the giants.

That was a question Jack couldn't answer, and so he abandoned the idea. His next plan was to challenge them to a fight — him against them, with no holds barred. They sportingly accepted the challenge and untied him. Then they tied him up again, and that was the end of that.

With plan number three he pretended to be dead. He reckoned they would untie him and throw him away, so he lay very still in his box.

"Definitely dead," said Klottid.

"Dead as a Cornish giant," said Kreem.

Jack's heart fluttered with hope.

"He's starting to smell already," said Klottid.

"We'll throw him on the fire straight away," said Kreem.

Jack miraculously came back to life, and that was the end of plan three.

Obviously these Devon giants were a lot less stupid than Cornish giants. They were making a fortune. They'd scared any other giant-killers out of Devon, and they seemed to have made escape impossible. What was needed was a super plan. And a super plan is what Jack eventually found.

Like all the best ideas, it was simple, though unlike all the best ideas, it did have one tiny flaw. The plan was to do nothing. One day, as Jack correctly reasoned, the giants would die and then someone might come and release him. Not only was this his best chance, but it was also his only chance, and so Jack settled down for a long wait.

The one tiny flaw in Jack's plan showed itself just twenty years later. Instead of the giants dying, it was Jack who died. This was quite unexpected, and he would have been rather upset about it if he had still been alive. Nobody knew exactly what he had died of, so the doctor wrote that the cause of death was Loss of Life, which seemed to cover everthing. The giants duly untied him and threw him away — as he had foreseen in plan three — but being untied and being free was not much use to him now that he was dead.

When news of his death eventually reached Charlotte, she took his dinner out of the oven and ate it herself.

"Twenty-one years I've been keeping it warm for him," she told her father, "and I'm certainly not going to waste it now."

As for the giants, they lived on for another twenty years, and finally died of old age, both on the same day. Their friends erected a tombstone for them, on which was written:

> *Here lie the giants, Klottid and Kreem,*
> *Who earned their place in Heaven*
> *By making sure that giant-killers*
> *Never killed in Devon.*

And since that time, no giant has ever been killed by a giant-killer in Devon.

Cinderella's Coachman

he trouble with having a good time is afterwards.
hen you've had a bad time, at least you can look
rward to things getting better, but when you've had
good time, you can only look forward to looking
ack. Robbie the Rat had such a good time as
inderella's coachman that he never looked forward
ain.

When the clock struck midnight, Cinderella's coach
rned back into a pumpkin, the horses turned back
to mice, and Robert the Coachman was once more
obbie the Rat. He'd had the greatest day of his life,
d he couldn't wait to tell everyone his story. He
ced back to the family home in the sewer.

"Phew, what a pong!" he exclaimed. "How can you rats bear to live in such filth?"

"What d'you mean 'you rats'?" snapped his father, cuffing him round the right ear.

"What d'you mean 'filth'?" snapped his mother, cuffing him round the left ear.

"And where have you been all night?" they both snapped together.

"You're never going to believe this story!" said Robbie.

"Then you'd better tell us another," said his father.

"But every word of it's true," said Robbie. "Just listen to what happened to me."

Then he told them all about Cinderella and the fairy godmother and the ball at the Prince's palace.

"There was this amazing disco!" he said. "And us coachmen, we were outside dancing and drinking and telling funny stories. I tell you, these human beings really know how to enjoy themselves. And food? Oof! I ate more goodies tonight than you rats can lay your paws on in a year. Anyway, I'm just starting to tell

them my favourite story about how I knocked out old Tom Cat in the tenth round when . . . boing! The clock strikes twelve and I turn into a rat again. What a comedown. One moment I'm swapping stories with them, and the next I'm staring them in the bootlaces and someone's shouting, 'Get that dirty rat!' Well, I just ran all the way home, and here I am."

Robbie was right: nobody believed him. Some of the rats exchanged knowing looks, one or two raised their paws and tapped their heads, and his father gave him a thrashing for telling a pack of lies.

"It's not lies!" wailed Robbie. "It's all true!"

Then his father gave him another thrashing for telling lies about his lies. Everyone in the sewer agreed that it was the most ridiculous story since the Pied Piper of Hamelin, but Robbie went on insisting that it was true. And as time went by, even his father eventually stopped calling him a liar.

"I was wrong," said Father Rat. "Robbie's not a liar. He's just plain bonkers."

A whole series of jokes went round the sewers:

Who left home ratty and came home batty?

Who went right in the palace and wrong in the head?

Who comes here and is never all there?

Who drove six horses and went round the bend?

Robbie's parents sent him to see Dr Whiskas, the famous neuratologist, who declared that Robbie was as nutty as marzipan, and that the only thing to do was to knock him on the head and hope for the best.

Dr Whiskas duly knocked Robbie on the head, and Robbie hit him back, and the two of them finished on the floor, each hitting the other on the head. Robbie won the fight on points, and Dr Whiskas went off to have his head examined.

It was clear that Robbie could have no future in the sewer, and so he resolved that from now on he would be a coachman or nothing. Even his parents were glad to see him go.

"Good riddance to bad rodents!" said his father.

But it was one thing to leave the sewer, and quite another to become a coachman. How *do* you become a coachman if you haven't got a coach and you aren't a man? The fairy godmother would know the answer, but where was she? Perhaps she'd be in Cinderella's house, for that, after all, was the place where it had all begun.

Robbie found the house quite easily, but of the fairy godmother and of Cinderella, there was no sign. The only people in the house were three women — one older and two younger and none of them very nice to look at or listen to.

"If you didn't have such big feet," the older one was saying, "you'd have got into that slipper!"

"It's not our fault we've got big feet!" grumbled one of the daughters.

"Big feet and ugly faces!" said the mother.

"We're not ugly," mumbled the other daughter. "At least, *I'm* not."

"Then why did he dance with Cinderella and not with you?" snapped the mother.

"Because he's obviously got a thing about small feet," said the second daughter.

Robbie left them quarrelling and set off for the only other place where his dream might come true — the scene of his greatest hours, the Prince's Palace. But when he got there, he found to his surprise that everything was very quiet — no coaches, no music, no dancing. He began to wonder whether perhaps he really had dreamt it all. Or could it be that the rats back home were right and he'd gone off his head?

("Who's the ratter that's mad as a hatter?" "Robbie the Coachman!")

Robbie wandered sadly through an open door, and found himself in a big hall. At the end of the hall, sitting on a throne and reading a book of fairytales, sat Cinderella.

With a whoop of delight, Robbie raced across the hall, skidding the last ten yards, and came to a halt right beside Cinderella's throne.

"Ahem!" he said. "Excuse me, Cinderella."

At least, that's what he thought he said. But the sound that came to Cinderella's ears was, "Squeak, squeak!" She looked down, and saw a rat sitting on the floor next to her throne.

"Hullo," she said.

Some princesses would not have said hullo. Some princesses would have said "Aaaargh!" jumped on to their thrones and screamed for help. But Cinderella liked animals, and besides, her home-life had taught her that some rats can be nicer than some people.

"I used to be your coachman," said Robbie. (Squeak, squeak!)

"I used to have a coachman like you," said Cinderella.

"I brought you to the Palace," said Robbie. (Squeak, squeak!)

"He brought me to the Palace," said Cinderella.

"Please can you tell me where to find the fairy godmother who turned me into a coachman?" asked Robbie. (Squeak, squeak, squeak!)

"My fairy godmother turned him into a coachman," said Cinderella.

Poor Robbie. The rats who understood him didn't believe him, and Cinderella, who would have believed him, didn't understand him. He explained everything slowly, he explained everything loudly, he waved his feet, he waggled his whiskers, he jumped up and down, he imitated the coachman, the horses, the fairy godmother, the dancing . . .

"Oh, dear," said Cinderella, "you are a peculiar rat. Well, thank you very much for the show, but I'm afraid I must be going now. I've got to explain to the cook how to make pumpkin pie."

"Don't go!" screamed Robbie. "Tell me where to find the fairy godmother." (Squeak, squeak!)

"What a funny rat," said Cinderella to herself as she left the hall. "I'm glad my coachman wasn't like that. I'd never have got to the Palace."

Robbie never found the fairy godmother, and as far as anyone knows, he's still searching. Even if he found her, of course, it wouldn't do him much good to be turned back into a coachman, since there are no more coaches for him to drive. But perhaps if the fairy godmother happens to read this account, she might still give the story a happy ending. All she would have to do is wave her magic wand and turn Robbie into a taxi-driver.

The Return of Rumpel What's-a-Name

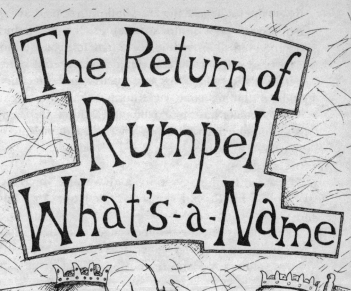

"Gold!" shouted the King. "I must have more gold!"

The Queen didn't say a word.

"I've filled this room with straw for you," said the King, "so now would you kindly spin it into gold."

"I can't," said the Queen.

"Yes, you can," said the King.

"No, I can't," said the Queen.

"You did it before!" shouted the King, going red in he face.

"No, I didn't," said the Queen, going white in the ace. "Rumpelstiltskin did."

Then she told the King the whole story: how, when she'd been a poor miller's daughter, the dwarf had spun the gold for her, but she'd had to promise him her first baby. Then the dwarf had said she could keep her baby if she guessed his name, and a messenger had found out that his name was Rumpelstiltskin.

"I need never have married you!" shouted the King. "I should have married Rumple what's-a-name!"

"Sorry," said the Queen. "If I'd realized, I'd have introduced you."

"How am I going to get my gold?" wailed the King. "Where is this Rumpleskin now, eh? How can I find him?"

The Queen sent for the messenger who had found the hut, and the messenger was despatched with twenty soldiers to capture the dwarf and bring him back to the palace.

Meanwhile, Rumpelstiltskin was sitting at home tearing his hair and gnashing his teeth. All his life he'd longed to be a father, but being ridiculously small and absurdly ugly, he'd never found anyone short-sighted enough to marry him. Then at last his chance had come, and he'd blown it. He'd even made a golden cot and a golden playpen and a golden pram and a golden chair. He'd covered his hut with bright decorations, and he'd made clothes for the baby to wear and toys for the baby to play with. All for nothing! He would spend the rest of his life alone, cursing his moment of weakness.

"If only I'd asked her to spell it instead of just guess it!" he howled.

When the soldiers arrived, Rumpelstiltskin was still wiping his eyes, but when they burst into his hut without even ringing the bell, he was very angry indeed.

"We've come from the Palace," said the first soldier.

"Then you can jolly well go back to the Palace!" screamed Rumpelstiltskin. And to help the soldiers on their way, he sent two of them rolling with a rolling-pin, poked two of them through the door with a poker, and knocked four of them flying with a frying-pan. But at last the soldiers overpowered him, and he was carried kicking and screaming before His Majesty, the King.

"Now then, Rubberskin," said the King, "I understand you can spin gold out of straw."

"My name's not Rubberskin!" shouted Rumpelstiltskin.

"Call yourself what you like," said the King. "It's gold I'm after. Here's a room full of straw, so get weaving."

"I won't!" shouted Rumpelstiltskin.

"Don't be silly," said the King. "I'm the King! Everybody obeys the King!"

"Then more fool everybody," shouted Rumpelstiltskin.

"If you don't weave my gold," said the King, "I'll chop off your head."

"If you chop off my head," said Rumpelstiltskin, "then how shall I weave your gold?"

The King said "oh" and "ah" and "um", he hadn't thought of that, and perhaps he had been a little hasty, and, er, what would Mr Rumandsoftdrinks like in return for the gold?

"I'll give you a room full of gold," said Rumpelstiltskin, "if you'll give me your baby daughter."

"What baby daughter?" asked the King.

One of the counsellors reminded him that the baby had been born a few weeks ago.

"Is that the thing that keeps going *Waa Waa* in the night?" asked the King.

"Yes, Your Majesty," replied the counsellor.

"You're welcome to that, then," said the King. "And good riddance!"

But when the Queen heard what had been arranged, she burst into tears and said that if the baby went, she would go too.

"What a good idea!" said the King.

"Not such a good idea," said Rumpelstiltskin.

But then the Queen explained to him all about breast-feeding, and getting up in the night, and changing nappies, and Rumpelstiltskin said that even if it wasn't such a good idea, it wasn't such a bad idea either. And so he spun a roomful of gold for the King, and next day set off for home with the Queen and the baby. The Queen, in fact, was quite pleased to leave the Palace because, being a poor miller's daughter, she had found palace life a bit of a grind.

The three of them settled down happily in the hut, and indeed Rumpelstiltskin was so delighted to have a family at last that he never once lost his temper but became kinder and gentler with every day that passed. The Queen soon forgot how small and ugly he was, and the Princess never even noticed it in the first place.

They lived in the hut for sixteen years, by which time the Princess had grown very beautiful, very intelligent, and very bored.

"It's not that I don't like our little home," she would say, "but it's not very exciting, is it?"

"Who wants excitement?" asked the Queen.

"I do," said the Princess.

"What sort of excitement?" asked Rumpelstiltskin.

But as the Princess didn't know what sort of excitement there was, that would put an end to the conversation and they'd all go off to sleep, which certainly wasn't very exciting.

Now, it so happened that at that very time the King was in his royal bed, dying of gold fever. And so while the Princess was trying to liven up, the King was trying to calm down, because as he lay on his deathbed his mind was very troubled indeed. This was partly because he was worried about his gold. His counsellors kept telling him, "You can't take it with you."

"In that case," said the King, "I'm not going."

But he *was* going, and the weaker he became, the more his conscience began to prick him. He remembered his wife and baby daughter, and he wished he'd been kinder to them. So he sent a messenger to the hut in the woods with a request that the Queen should bring their daughter to the Palace in order that he could say hullo and goodbye to them.

The Princess was excited at the invitation to the palace, the Queen didn't want to go but felt sorry for the King, and Rumpelstiltskin said that as it was a request, and not an order, they ought to go. So off they all went to the Palace.

The King was very pleased to see them — especially his beautiful daughter.

"My, how you've grown!" he said.

"Nonsense!" said Rumpelstiltskin.

"Not you," said the King. "My daughter! And as for you, my dear . . ." he turned his face towards the Queen, "will you forgive me for sending you away?"

"It was the nicest thing you ever did for me," said the Queen.

Then the King asked the Queen to stay in the Palace and be Queen again, but the Queen said she'd rather not, thank you.

"If I were Queen," said the Princess, "could I live in the Palace?"

"Yes," said the King.

"Right then, I'll be Queen," said the Princess.

"What a good idea," said the King. "Now I can die happy. Just one more thing . . ."

His voice was very weak, but he managed to flap his hand feebly towards Rumpelstiltskin. "Rumbletum-tum..."

Rumpelstiltskin approached the royal bed, and stood on tiptoe to hear the King's last words:

"Would you be a good fellow . . . get all my gold together . . . and make me . . . a gold coffin?"

"It'll be a pleasure," said Rumpelstiltskin.

"Thank Heavens," said the King. "Then I can . . . take it with me after all."

And so the King died and was buried in a gold coffin, the Princess became Queen, the ex-Queen and Rumpelstiltskin went back to their hut in the woods, and they all lived happily ever after. Except, of course, the King.

How to Catch Three Little Pigs

Hi there! I'm Wilfie — Wolfie's brother. Wolfie's the one that got blown to bits by Granny, which was a pretty stupid thing to do. You won't catch me in some old woman's bed, I can tell you. No, I'm the smart wolf that caught the three little pigs. You remember the first part of the story? The first little pig built a straw house, and I huffed and I puffed till I blew his house down. But he ran away. The second little pig built a house of grass and reeds, and I huffed and I puffed till I blew his house down. But he ran away, too. Then the third little pig built a brick house, and I huffed and I puffed till I needed an air transfusion. His house just wouldn't fall, so I climbed down the chimney and landed in a stew pot. All I got was a very hot bot, and *I* ran away.

But we wolves don't give up that easily. Besides, there was a meat shortage at the time, so those three little pigs were my best chance of having a future. By now they were all living together in the brick house, so either I had to lure them outside, or I had to sneak my way inside.

My first idea was to invite them to a barbecue. What I had in mind was barbecued pig, but I didn't tell them that. Instead, I sent them a very clever invitation:

The Lord Mayor requests the pleasure of the company of
THE THREE LITTLE PIGS
at a grand barbecue in Farmer Giles' field
on Saturday the 4th at 6 p.m.

R.S.V.P.

My plan was to get to the field at 5.55 p.m. and jump on the first little pig to come through the gate. Good thinking, eh? The invitation looked really official, and that 'R.S.V.P.' was the master stroke. I didn't know what it meant, but people always put it at the end of invitations, and it looked good.

At 5.55 p.m. I was nicely hidden behind Farmer Giles' gate. I stayed there for three and a half hours, and not a single pig came to the field. I was furious. I mean, if you get an invitation like that, you don't just ignore it, do you? I had a good mind to complain to the Lord Mayor. However, when I read the newspaper the next day, I decided not to. It said that the Lord Mayor was looking for someone who'd been sending invitations in his name. And whoever it was would be severely punished.

I later found out that R.S.V.P. is a funny way of saying 'please reply'. The three little pigs had written to the Lord Mayor to tell him they'd love to come to his barbecue, and the Lord Mayor had written back to say, "What barbecue?"

My next idea was to use my talents as an actor. I am in fact a master of disguise, and I dressed myself up as an old woman. I put on a bonnet, a pair of spectacles, a long frilly dress, and I carried a basket over one arm. Then I walked down the street crying: "Truffles! Who'll buy my truffles?" I wanted the pigs to hear me in the distance so that they'd think it really was a truffle-seller. Unfortunately, several people came out of their houses to buy my truffles, and as I hadn't got any they said some rather nasty things and the scene turned ugly. I had to use up a lot of huff and puff to get away.

But I didn't give up the truffle plan. I just changed my tactics. I waited an hour or so, then I crept down the street till I reached the brick house, and I knocked on the door. A little piggy face peeped through the curtain, and a little piggy voice asked, "Who is it?"

This was my big moment. I perched the spectacles on the end of my nose, and in a high cracked voice, just like an old woman's, I called out: "I'm a poor old woman, and I'm selling lovely truffles. Won't you open your door, my dear, and try a truffle?"

It was a superb performance. Not only did I look like an old woman, not only did I sound like an old woman, but I even felt like an old woman.

"Go away, Wilfie," said the little pig. "We don't want your truffles, and we won't open our door."

Someone must have tipped them off. How else would they have known?

With my next idea, I didn't see how anything could possibly go wrong. It was simple, but ingenious. I knocked at their door (as myself this time — no disguises at all) and called out, "Little pigs, little pigs, please help me! I'm dying! Please open your door and help me!"

Of course I knew they wouldn't open the door. They were smart, those pigs, and that's why I had to be super-smart to catch them.

A little piggy face peeped through the curtain, and a little piggy voice said: "Go away, Wilfie. We're not going to open our door."

It was time for another great bit of acting.

"I'm dying, piggy," I groaned. "Oh . . . ah . . . the pain! All I ask is a glass of water. Nothing more. Water, before I . . . ah . . . oh . . . die!"

"Let us know when you've finished dying, Wilfie!" said one little piggy voice.

"And don't forget to invite the Lord Mayor to your funeral!" said another.

Then there were three little piggy giggles, but I didn't mind that at all. My time would come.

"Ah . . . oh . . . ee!" I groaned. "Everything's . . . going dark . . . I can't see . . . I can't hear . . ." etc. etc.

I kept it up for several minutes, making my voice weaker and weaker, and at last with a despairing cry of "Aaargh!" I slid down their door and collapsed in a heap on the ground. And there I lay, still and stiff, with just one eye half open so that I could see what was going on. They would all cry, "Hurrah, he's dead!" and do a dance of joy round their living room. Then they would peep through their curtain to make sure, and after that, they would open their door to have a good look at dead Wilfie, and then . . .

Still and stiff I lay. Hour after hour. It began to rain. Big, cold, wet drops. I got soaked through. Night began to fall. No pigs. Well, I tell you, I very nearly did die that night. When at last I gave up, I could hardly even stand, I was so wet and cold. It took me a whole week in bed to recover. Those pigs had no feelings. In fact, as I limped away from their piggy little home that night, I thought I actually heard them giggling.

After an experience like that, most wolves would have given up, but I was determined. I was also hungry. And this time I had a plan that simply couldn't (and didn't) fail. It was so brilliant that even now I have to admire myself for it. So stand by while I tell you exactly how I caught the three little pigs.

As everybody knows, pigs like mud. Mud-bathing for a pig is like pig-eating for a wolf — sheer enjoyment. So I ordered a ton of mud (at great expense) and had it all tipped in their front garden. Then I knocked at their door. A little piggy face peeped through the curtain, and a little piggy voice giggled, "Oh look, it's the ghost of Wilfie!"

"Hello, little pigs," I said. "I'm going away and I wanted to make up with you before I left. So I've brought you a mud-pudding as a goodbye present."

"Thank you, goodbye, and good riddance," said the little pig.

Of course I knew they wouldn't come out until I'd gone, so I said, "Goodbye, little pigs. I shall be going far away, right up over the hill, but I do want us to part as friends. So when I'm up at the top of that hill, please wave to me, and then I'll know you like me as much as I like you."

Off I went. It took me twenty minutes to puff my way up that hill, but when I got there I looked down at the little pigs' house in the distance. And there they were, at their open front door. I gave them a cheery wave, and they all waved back. Then with little oinks of delight, into the mud-pudding they dived. And in the mud-pudding they stuck. Because before it was delivered, I'd mixed the mud with Superstick Golden Goose Glue. Sheer genius! So that was how I finally caught the three little pigs.

Unfortunately, the story doesn't quite end there. I strolled down the hill, laughing quietly to myself, and when I reached the pigs' front garden, all three were terrified.

"Got you, my little beauties," I said. "Ho, ho, bacon for my breakfast, pork for my lunch, and trotters for my supper. Yum yum."

"Please don't eat us, Wilfie!" they cried.

"Sorry, my dears," I said. "But if I'm to keep the wolf from the door, so to speak, it's you that will . . . ho ho . . . save my bacon."

I really was in tremendous form.

Licking my lips, and with jaws almost aching in anticipation, I bounded towards the little pigs. But one bound was all I managed. After that, I couldn't move. I was stuck fast – in Superstick Golden Goose Glue.

The rest of the story is rather sad, and I'll tell it as briefly as possible. Farmer Giles came along, rescued the three little pigs, and shot me dead.

All the same, I did catch those three little pigs, didn't I? I outsmarted them, and it was just sheer bad luck that I outsmarted myself as well. And it's certainly true to say that any wolf that could outsmart me must have been a very smart wolf.

Betsy Byars
The Not-Just Anybody Family £1.95

Meet the Blossoms – a family to follow

BOY BREAKS INTO CITY JAIL

It made all the headlines when Vern broke *into* prison, but what would you do if your grandpa was in jail? The Blossoms had no doubts. Since they couldn't get Pap out, Maggie and Vern had to get in. A little unusual, perhaps, but as Maggie said, 'We Blossoms have never been just "anybody".'

This is the first adventure for the Blossoms – Pap, Vern, Maggie, Junior and Mud the dog. They're a family you won't forget.

Rose Tremain
Journey to the Volcano £1.95

'As they swam, their eyes stayed fixed on the volcano. The black cloud sat tight on its rim. Then, up through the black cloud and spurting high into the clear sky above it came a gush of flame, higher than any fountain, brighter than any firework . . .
  '"She's going!" cried Guido.'

Trouble had been brewing all summer, from the day George's mother left his father and snatched George from his London school. Escaping to his mother's old home on the slopes of Mount Etna, George found himself plunged into the heart of a large family he barely knew. Life on the mountain was exciting and different. But under the sunny slopes lay a seething mass of molten lava, waiting to erupt . . .

All Pan books are available at your local bookshop or newsagent, or can be ordered direct from the publisher. Indicate the number of copies required and fill in the form below.

Send to: **CS Department, Pan Books Ltd., P.O. Box 40,
             Basingstoke, Hants.   RG21 2YT.**

or phone: 0256 469551 (Ansaphone), quoting title, author
             and Credit Card number.

Please enclose a remittance* to the value of the cover price plus: 60p for the first book plus 30p per copy for each additional book ordered to a maximum charge of £2.40 to cover postage and packing.

*Payment may be made in sterling by UK personal cheque, postal order, sterling draft or international money order, made payable to Pan Books Ltd.

Alternatively by Barclaycard/Access:

Card No.

_____
                         Signature:

Applicable only in the UK and Republic of Ireland.

While every effort is made to keep prices low, it is sometimes necessary to increase prices at short notice. Pan Books reserve the right to show on covers and charge new retail prices which may differ from those advertised in the text or elsewhere.

NAME AND ADDRESS IN BLOCK LETTERS PLEASE:

....

Name _____

Address _____

_____

_____

_____

                                                        3/87